Books by the same author

Crumbling Castle

Picture Books

The Cats of Tiffany Street
Eat Up, Gemma
The Grumpalump
Lucy Anna and the Finders
Mary, Mary
Nine Ducks Nine
This Is the Bear
This Is the Bear and the Bad Little Girl
This Is the Bear and the Picnic Lunch
This Is the Bear and the Scary Night

Action Books

Clap Your Hands
Stamp Your Feet

EASY PEASY

"When long becomes short
And small becomes tall,
No one will trouble
Amazing Sam Small."

This is the message given to Sam Small by his new friends. But what does it mean? And how can it help Sam, the smallest boy in the school, with his big troubles?

Sarah Hayes says that "a story is something made up but some of the things that go into it are real." Sam is based on her own son Felix, who was small, and the circus stunts are things that she saw and wished she could do. Her numerous stories for children include the *This Is the Bear* books, *Crumbling Castle*, *The Grumpalump* and *Eat Up, Gemma*. She has also illustrated three of her own stories, *Nine Ducks Nine*, *The Cats of Tiffany Street* and *Lucy Anna and the Finders* (2000). Sarah Hayes has three children and lives in Oxfordshire.

John Bendall-Brunello comes from a family of eleven children. He has illustrated several children's books, including the Walker titles *The Big Bad Mole's Coming*, *When I Grow Bigger* and *Into the Castle*. He is married and lives in Cambridge.

SARAH HAYES

Illustrations by

John Bendall-Brunello

WALKER BOOKS
AND SUBSIDIARIES
LONDON • BOSTON • SYDNEY

For Sophie
S.H.

To my wife, Tiziana
J.B-B.

First published 1994 by
Walker Books Ltd, 87 Vauxhall Walk
London SE11 5HJ

This edition published 1995

6 8 10 9 7 5

Text © 1994 Sarah Hayes
Illustrations © 1994 John Bendall-Brunello

This book has been typeset in ITC Garamond Light.

Printed in England by Clays Ltd, St Ives plc

British Library Cataloguing in Publication Data
A catalogue record for this book is
available from the British Library.

ISBN 0-7445-3688-X

CONTENTS

THE MESSAGE

Sam wasn't at school when the
battered yellow van arrived.
He should have been. But he
wasn't. He was sitting on the steps
outside his flat. The van stopped
and a woman got out. She had
short purple hair.

The woman opened the back of the van and three silver skittles rolled onto the pavement. Then a tall man in a hat got out. He was holding a baby wearing shoes with bells on them.

Sam jumped down the steps, picked up the skittles and put them back in the van.

The man bowed. "Hold Piglet a minute," he said, and handed Sam the baby. Sam had never held a baby before.

The man took off his hat and tipped out three puffy gold stars and two gold moons. Then he threw them all into the air and caught them one by one. Round his head, through his legs, behind his back went the stars and the moons. "Joe Juggles," the man said. "At your service."

Catch a falling star.

"Dropped it," said the baby. But the stars and moons went on whirling round and round.

The woman with the purple hair put her hand to her mouth and made a noise like someone playing a trumpet.

"Toots, the Human Trumpet," said Joe.

"I'm Sam," said Sam. He took a deep breath. "Sam Small."

Joe Juggles didn't laugh. He didn't even smile. He caught the stars and moons in his hat and said, "Now that is a very useful name."

"Not if you're the smallest boy in the school," said Sam.

Joe sat down on the top step and took Piglet onto his knee.

Sam jumped up the steps, all four of them at once.

"Do that again," said Toots.

"Easy peasy," said Sam. He jumped down and then back up. Toots nodded but she didn't say anything. So Sam sat down next to Joe and told him about being the smallest boy in the school. It was trouble. It was three kinds of trouble.

Trouble with the dinner ladies.

Trouble with the big girls.

Trouble with horrible Beany Bennett.

When Sam had finished, Joe stood up. "What do you think, Toots?" he said.

Toots didn't reply. Instead she stood on her head.

"Don't worry," said Joe. "Just be quiet and wait."

Sam waited. And waited. And then it came. Toots's lips were moving, but it wasn't Toots's voice. It wasn't the Human Trumpet either. This is what it said:

When long becomes short
And small becomes tall,
No one will trouble
Amazing Sam Small.

"It's a message," said Joe. "You don't have to do a thing."

Toots turned the right way up and said, "Come and see us tomorrow, Sam, when we're unpacked. It's not very far. Just up the stairs."

And that was the day that Joe Juggles, Toots the Human Trumpet and Baby Piglet moved into the upstairs flat – the day things began to change for Sam Small.

LONG BECOMES SHORT

Next morning Sam took a cake
upstairs.

The door was slightly open, but
Sam didn't know whether to go in.
Then he saw Joe.

Joe took the cake and picked
up a stick. Then he spun the plate
on the top of the stick and put the
bottom of the stick on his nose.

Toots came in. "It's a big mistake to juggle cake," she said.

Joe stepped backwards and bumped into a blow-up gorilla.

The plate flew off the stick.

Sam jumped and caught the plate as it came down. But the cake slid off and landed on his head.

Toots scooped off a lump.

Joe helped himself to a bit of cake.

Sam just stood there. It felt funny
having people eating off the top of
your head.

"Sam Small, the Human Plate," Sam said, and they all got the giggles. A drip of chocolate reached the corner of Sam's mouth. He licked it off.

Joe unhooked a giant wooden spoon from the wall and Toots fetched a teaspoon.

They were scraping the last of the cake off Sam's head when Piglet staggered in. She was holding a huge rabbit.

"Meet Snowflake," said Joe. "A conjuror gave her to us. She got too big for his hat."

The baby and the rabbit sat down very suddenly. "Dropped it," said Piglet.

The huge pile of fluff hopped towards Sam. Then it stood on its hind legs and nibbled the chocolate in his hair.

Toots said that was Snowflake's way of saying that Sam needed a hair wash.

Usually Sam hated having his hair washed. But this time it was all right.

Joe filled a big china bowl with warm water and Sam knelt on the rug. Toots blew bubbles through her fingers and Piglet splashed water everywhere. The drying was all right too, because they used Snowflake's heavy-duty hairdryer. But as it dried, Sam's hair got curlier and curlier and more and more knotted.

Sam looked at the tangled mess in the mirror and he made a decision.

Toots had a chat with Sam's mum, who wasn't very happy. But in the end she agreed.

And so Joe did it, with his
special clippers and a Grade Three
attachment.

When he had finished, Sam looked completely different. He felt different too, sort of light and bouncy.

For the rest of the day Sam and his mum kept running their hands over the soft fuzz which now covered his head.

When he was in bed Sam realized that the first part of his message had come true.

When long becomes short
And small becomes tall,
No one will trouble
Amazing Sam Small.

His hair had been long. And now it was short.

But what about the rest of the message?

SMALL BECOMES TALL

Sam was still in his pyjamas when
Toots rang the bell next morning.

"Time to go to work," she said.
"We'll collect you in five minutes.
And it's OK with your mum. We
checked last night."

Sam sat in the back of the van with Joe and Piglet, and Toots drove. The van had all sorts of stuff clipped to the sides.

After a long time they stopped in a square with cafés and stalls all round it. On the far side was a big building with pillars. Something black was stuck between two of the pillars, almost at the top.

As they got closer Sam could
see that the black thing was a man
braced between the pillars. By
moving one hand and then one foot
and then another hand and another
foot he was slowly climbing up the
pillars. It looked very dangerous.

There were only a few people watching Fly, but Joe said it was early yet. You had to be there early to get a good pitch. Sam helped unload the van.

Fly climbed down and came over to say hello. Sam thought he looked pretty silly. But Piglet loved him.

While Joe set up the pitch, Fly played with Piglet, and Toots and Sam went off to the park to practise. First they did this:

And then this:

And then this, which was a lot harder:

Toots said that was called a flic-flac and not many people could do it. "You're a born tumbler, Sam," she said. "You've got natural bounce."

When they got back to the square, there were loads of people there. Toots lifted Sam up so he could see over the crowd round their pitch. Joe was riding a unicycle and juggling with a watch, a grapefruit and a baseball cap.

Sam and Toots squeezed through to the front – Joe was still juggling. Toots worked round the ring on her hands and did a bit of Human Trumpeting. People clapped even more. Then Toots pinched her nose and said in a loudspeaker voice:

Would the owners of a watch, a grapefruit and a baseball cap kindly come and collect their property.

Three people from the audience came into the ring and Joe gave them back their things. Then he picked up Piglet and went round with a hat and most people put money in it. When he got to Sam, Joe winked at him and whispered,

"Picnic time." Then he emptied the hat into a lock-up box in his suitcase, and Toots said, "That's it, folks," and the crowd went off to look at someone else's act.

Sam didn't eat much picnic.
He was too nervous. Because…
In the afternoon, after a bit of
practising, a new act joined
Joe Juggles and Toots the Human
Trumpet.

At the end of the performance,
just before the hat went round,
Toots said in her loudspeaker voice:
"And now, for his first public
appearance, will you welcome an

exciting new tumbler. Please put
your hands together for the boy
with natural bounce… Sam Small!"
Toots did a drum roll and Sam
flic-flacked across the ring.

Then Toots walked round on her hands and Sam cartwheeled and Joe cycled round on the unicycle. The best came last. Toots did a really slow drum roll, and Joe leant down from the unicycle and caught hold of Sam's hands. Sam bounced and Joe lifted. And then he was standing on Joe's shoulders. Round and round the ring they went. People roared and whistled and clapped.

Then Sam jumped down and took
the hat round. He collected loads.
Joe put it with the rest in the lock-up
box in the suitcase.

It was the best day of Sam's life.
And he got paid!

When they were driving home Sam remembered his message.

When long becomes short
And small becomes tall,
No one will trouble
Amazing Sam Small.

Another bit of the message had come true. Riding round on Joe's shoulders on the unicycle, Sam Small really had become tall.

Then he remembered something else. Tomorrow was Monday. And that meant school. A whole week of it.

AMAZING SAM SMALL

Dinner break was always the worst.
They were all there – the dinner
ladies, the big girls and horrible
Beany Bennett. Three kinds of
trouble. Sam dawdled about as long
as he could, but in the end he had
to go out into the playground.

Usually the dinner ladies called
him back to pinch his cheek and
ruffle his curls. But today he didn't
have any curls to ruffle. And today
the dinner ladies let him go past.

Sam put his head down and
walked towards the mound. That
way he might miss the big girls.
They said the mound was only for
little kids. But in the playground the
big girls were waiting for Sam. And
they didn't want to ruffle his curls.

They wanted to pick him up and feel his Grade Three haircut. They thought it was sweet! The biggest of the big girls tried to lift him up, but Sam dived out of her arms into a forward flip. He followed this with two perfect cartwheels and three flic-flacs. The big girls clapped.

Do it again, Sam!

Sam did it again. Lots of people
clapped this time.

A loudspeaker voice boomed
across the playground:

And now will you welcome
the boy with natural bounce...
Amazing Sam Small.

And there was Toots, standing
with Joe and Piglet on the other side
of the playground wall.

Sam grinned and waved. Everyone
clapped again.

But then, from round the back of the boiler shed, came Beany Bennett. When he saw Sam he stopped and stared.

Everyone began to say it. "Samantha Small, Samantha Small, Samantha Small's not very tall."

Sam took a deep breath, bent his knees and began to flic-flac towards Benny Bennett. One … two … three … four … five flic-flacs.

When he reached Beany, Sam stared straight into his horrible little eyes.

"Hold out your hands," Sam said. Beany was so surprised that he held out his hands without thinking.

Sam took hold of Beany's hands. "Lift when I say lift," said Sam.

Beany was so surprised that he nodded.

Sam bounced and Beany lifted.

Now Sam stood on Beany's shoulders.

"Walk!" said Sam.

Beany was so surprised that he walked.

A slow drum roll came from the other side of the playground wall. Round and round the playground they walked. Everyone roared and stamped and whistled and clapped.

Then Beany began to stagger so
Sam jumped down and whispered,
"Bow!" and they both bowed.

"Blimey," said Beany Bennett.
And he actually grinned at Sam.
Sam grinned back.

The loudspeaker voice boomed:

Will you welcome
the exciting new double act—
Big Beany Bennett
and Amazing Sam Small.

There was more clapping and
then the voice changed:

When long becomes short
And small becomes tall,
No one will trouble
Amazing Sam Small.

And no one ever did.

MORE WALKER SPRINTERS
For You to Enjoy

☐ 0-7445-3091-1   *The Finger-eater*
by Dick King-Smith/Arthur Robins   £3.99

☐ 0-7445-3687-1   *Hector the Rat*
by Tony Wilkinson   £3.99

☐ 0-7445-3664-2   *Gemma and the Beetle People*
by Enid Richemont/Tony Kenyon   £3.99

☐ 0-7445-3665-0   *The Biggest Birthday Card in the World*
by Alison Morgan/Carolyn Dinan   £3.99

☐ 0-7445-3196-9   *Captain Cranko and the Crybaby*
by Jean Ure/Mick Brownfield   £3.50

☐ 0-7445-3666-9   *Beware the Killer Coat*
by Susan Gates/Josip Lizatović   £3.50

☐ 0-7445-3668-5   *Impossible Parents*
by Brian Patten/Arthur Robins   £3.50

☐ 0-7445-3667-7   *Taking the Cat's Way Home*
by Jan Mark/Paul Howard   £3.50